Teeny, Tiny
MOUSE
A BOOK ABOUT COLORS

For my wonderful parents, John and Gwen—L.L.

For the very colorful Thomas family!—P.S.

Teeny, Tiny
MOUSE

A BOOK ABOUT COLORS

by Laura Leuck

illustrated by Pat Schories

BridgeWater Books

Text copyright © 1998 by Laura Leuck.

Illustrations copyright © 1998 by Pat Schories.

Published by BridgeWater Books, an imprint and registered trademark of
Troll Communications L.L.C.

Designed by Dorit Radandt.

Hand lettering by Dee Dee Burnside.

Printed in the United States of America.

10 9 8 7 6 5 4 3 2 1

Library of Congress Cataloging-in-Publication Data

Leuck, Laura.
   Teeny, tiny mouse / by Laura Leuck ; illustrated by Pat Schories.
     p. cm.
   Summary: A teeny, tiny mouse and his mommy point out objects of various colors all
around their teeny, tiny house.
   ISBN 0-8167-4547-1
   [1. Color–Fiction.   2. Mice–Fiction.   3. Stories in rhyme.]
I. Schories, Pat, ill.   II. Title.
PZ8.3.L565Te   1998
[E]–dc21
                                             97-30887

"Can you name some colors in our teeny, tiny house?"
said the teeny, tiny mommy to the teeny, tiny mouse.

"There are colored things in every room,
and I can name them, too.
Throughout our teeny, tiny house
I'll point them out to you."

"Can you name some blue things in our teeny, tiny house?"
said the teeny, tiny mommy to the teeny, tiny mouse.

"There's a blue chair in the parlor.
A blue picture on the wall.
And a teeny, tiny blue ball
rolling slowly down the hall."

"Can you name some brown things in our teeny, tiny house?"
said the teeny, tiny mommy to the teeny, tiny mouse.

"There's a brown clock on the mantel
and a brown rug on the floor.
And a teeny, tiny brown knob
on the teeny, tiny door."

"Can you name some black things in our teeny, tiny house?"
said the teeny, tiny mommy to the teeny, tiny mouse.

"There's a black pot on the table.
A black handle on a pan.
And some teeny, tiny black beans
in a teeny, tiny can."

"Can you name some orange things in our teeny, tiny house?"
said the teeny, tiny mommy to the teeny, tiny mouse.

"There's a pitcher full of orange juice.
Orange cheese for lunch.
And some teeny, tiny flowers
in a teeny, tiny bunch."

"Can you name some red things in our teeny, tiny house?"
said the teeny, tiny mommy to the teeny, tiny mouse.

"There's a red bike in the corner.
A red cushion on its seat.
And teeny, tiny red shoes
for my teeny, tiny feet."

"Can you name some green things in our teeny, tiny house?"
said the teeny, tiny mommy to the teeny, tiny mouse.

"There's a green plant in the sunroom.
A green sweater that I wear.
And green teeny, tiny pillows
on the teeny, tiny chair."

"Can you name some pink things in our teeny, tiny house?"
said the teeny, tiny mommy to the teeny, tiny mouse.

"There's a pink hat on the bedpost
and pink lipstick on the stand.
And a teeny, tiny pink belt
with a teeny, tiny band."

"Can you name some white things in our teeny, tiny house?"
said the teeny, tiny mommy to the teeny, tiny mouse.

"There's a white frame 'round the mirror
and white handles on the tub.
And some teeny, tiny white soap
that I use to wash and scrub."

"Can you name some purple things
in our teeny, tiny house?"
said the teeny, tiny mommy
to the teeny, tiny mouse.

"There's a purple spread across my bed.
Purple stripes upon my walls.
And a teeny, tiny purple phone
for teeny, tiny calls."

"Can you name some yellow things
in our teeny, tiny house?"
said the teeny, tiny mommy
to the teeny, tiny mouse.

"There's a yellow roof above us
and a yellow floor below.
And a teeny, tiny candle
with a teeny, tiny glow."

"You have named the colors in our teeny, tiny house,"
said the teeny, tiny mommy to the teeny, tiny mouse.

"I know the colors one and all
as sure as I'm a mouse."

Do you know all the colors in
YOUR teeny, tiny house?

The Three Little

DINOSAURS

**Written
and Illustrated by
Jim Harris**

PELICAN PUBLISHING COMPANY
Gretna 1999

For Houston

*The word "Pelican" and the depiction of a pelican are trademarks
of Pelican Publishing Company, and are registered
in the U.S. Patent and Trademark Office.*

Library of Congress Cataloging-in-Publication Data

Harris, Jim, 1955-
      The three little dinosaurs / written and illustrated by
Jim Harris.
          p.   c.m.
    Summary: In this variation on the story of the Three Little
  Pigs, three young dinosaurs set out on their own, only to be
  hassled by a tyrannosaurus rex who gets a big surprise in the end.
      ISBN 1-56554-371-8 (hardcover : alk. paper)
      [1. Folklore.]   I. Three little pigs. English. II. Title.
    PZ8.1.H232Th 1999
  [398.2]—dc21
  [E]   99-23571
                                                            CIP

Printed in Korea

Published by Pelican Publishing Company, Inc.
1000 Burmaster Street, Gretna, Louisiana 70053

The Three Little Dinosaurs

Once upon a time in a thick, steamy jungle, there lived three little dinosaurs.

One day their mother called the little dinos in. "It is time you went out into the world and made it on your own," she said. "But be careful of the big bad Tyrannosaurus rex, or he will make dino-burgers out of you!"

The three dinosaurs giggled. "Right!" they said. And they headed out into the jungle.

The first little dinosaur wasn't into heavy construction work. He had better things to do. So he gathered some dried grass and quickly heaped it up into the shape of a house.

"This will do nicely," he said. He grabbed some snacks, plugged in his favorite video game, and plopped down in his comfy chair.

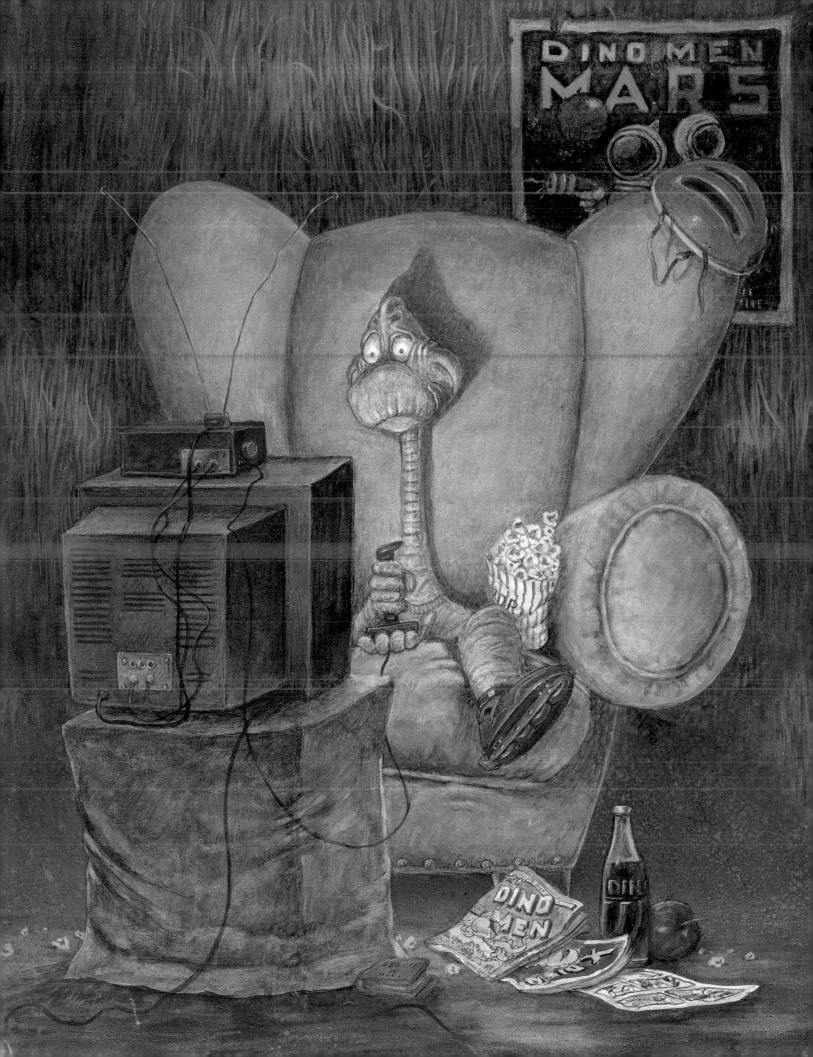

But before he could blow up the first alien ship, he heard a heavy *thump, thump, thump* coming up to his house.

"Who could that be?" he wondered. "Maybe it's the pizza deliveryman!"

But it wasn't the pizza deliveryman—it was the Tyrannosaurus rex. He smelled the little dino inside the straw hut, and his mouth watered. "Little pig, little pig, let me come in!" he growled.

"No way, José," the first little dino shouted back, "and *don't* call me a pig. I'm a dinosaur!"

"Then I'll huff, and I'll puff, and I'll blow your house in!" yelled the Rex.

And he huffed, and he puffed, and he blew the little grass hut to smithereens.

But in the confusion the first little dino snuck out and ran off to find his brothers.

The second little dino trudged through the hot jungle until he came to a Stegosaur sitting in a mud hole.

"What's happening?" asked the second little dinosaur.

"Making bricks," replied the Stegosaur.

"Mind if I have a few to build a house with?" asked the second little dino.

"Sure," the Steg said, "but you *must* let them dry for several days under the hot sun before they will be ready."

"Thanks!" cried the second little dino. And off he went with his mud bricks.

But the second little dino did *not* wait to dry the bricks. Instead, he went right ahead and stacked them up into a little house. No sooner had he finished, than the first little dino came running up.

"No problem!" the second little dino said after his brother told him about the Rex. "You can move in with me."

But the Rex had followed the first little dino to the mud brick house. He banged on the door.

"Little pigs, little pigs, let me come in," shouted the Rex. And he thought, *I'll make a* **double** *cheeseburger out of them.*

"Not by the hair of my chinny chin, chin," called out the second little dino. "Besides, you didn't say *please.*"

"And *stop* calling us pigs!" shouted the first little dino.

The Rex grinned a sharp, toothy grin. "Then I'll huff, and I'll puff, and I'll blow your house in!"

But he huffed, and he puffed, and he blew and blew, and the little house would not budge. Then he noticed the bricks were not quite dry. "Ahh!" he sighed. And he went and gathered some buckets of water.

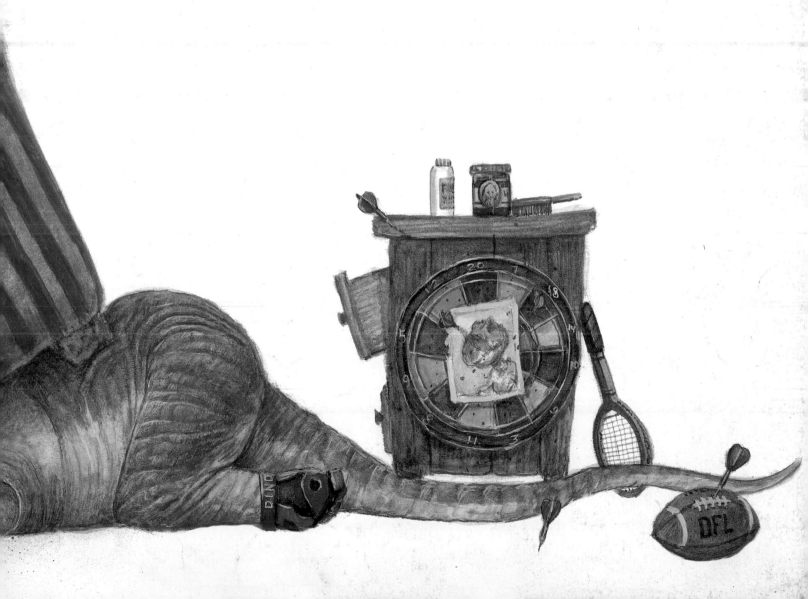

The Rex climbed up on top of the little house and started pouring water on the roof. At first the house began to sag. Then it drooped and dripped, until finally the soggy little house melted into a puddle of mud.

The Rex grabbed up the little dinos. But they were covered in wet, slimy mud, and they slipped out of the Rex's fingers and dashed into the forest. "I'll get those little pigs yet!" he growled, and set off to follow their muddy trail.

Meanwhile, the third little dino hiked through the tall, vine-covered trees until he came to an extinct volcano. The big rocks and boulders gave him an idea! Working very hard, he used the huge boulders to build the foundation and the smaller rocks to build the walls of his house. It was a *very large* and beautiful house. Which was good, because no sooner had he finished putting on the door hinges, than his two brothers came running up, panting and dripping with mud.

"Can . . . we stay . . . with . . . you?" they squeaked between breaths.

"You bet!" he said.

But the Rex was not far behind. "Little pigs, little pigs, let me come in!" he called.

"Hey, Rex, you really need a new opening line!" called back the second little dino.

"And stop calling us *pigs!*" shouted the first little dino.

"Then I'll huff, and I'll puff, and I'll blow your house in!" shouted back the Rex.

"I'm sooooo scared," laughed the third little dino, "you can't blow a rock house down. It's your bad breath that has *me* worried. Don't you ever brush?!"

This, of course, made the Rex very mad, so he huffed his very biggest huff. And he puffed his biggest puff. And he blew and he blew, 'til his tongue hung down to his chin. But nothing happened.

So he brought his buckets of water. And he poured, and poured, and poured some more. But he could not melt the house either.

But Rex wouldn't give up. Every night he sat up in his house long after bedtime, and thought and thought about how to get those three little dinos. Now, Rex had a brain the size of a peanut so it took him not days, not months, but *years,* 'til one night he finally thought of the answer.

"This is brilliant!" he shouted. He could just taste those piggy-burgers with mustard and melted cheese.

The next day Rex found a long pole and placed it carefully under a giant boulder on the peak of a tall mountain above the rock house. Then he pulled. And he **tugged**. And finally he **jumped** on the end of the pole.

The huge rock tilted over and began to roll. Faster and faster, it rolled down the side of the mountain, through the forest, across a creek, and then *SMASH!*

Right into the rock house.

"I've done it! I've done it!" he cried. And he raced down to what was left of the third dino's house to get a triple-deluxe burger for lunch.

But the three little dinos weren't there!

"Now where could those little porkers be?" he muttered.

He was busily looking for them under every rock and didn't notice somebody walk up behind him. "Who is going to pay for this?" demanded a gruff voice. "I hope you've got insurance, buster!"

"And stop calling us pigs!" added another, deeper voice.

"It's a good thing we were outside," drawled a third voice. "You could've hurt somebody, fella!"

The Rex grinned wickedly and turned around quickly to grab the little dinos before they could get away. But he found himself eye-to-eye with . . .

. . . a rather round belly!

While Rex had been trying to figure out how to get into the rock house, the little dinos had grown up and up and up! Rex looked up at the three great big dinos and turned very pale.

"Ahh . . . sorry about the house," he squeaked. "Uh, I just remembered, I gotta dentist appointment. Yeah, that's it, a dentist appointment."

Then he turned and ran as fast as he could, and didn't slow down 'til he was far, far away.

So the three brothers built new houses and lived happily ever after.

And they never saw hide nor hair of Rex again. Because he has taken up a quiet, more peaceful life—

He's gone fishing.